2/00

Never Let Your Cat Make Lunch for You

Lee Harris
Pictures by Debbie Tilley

TRICYCLE PRESS
Berkeley, California

Never let your cat make lunch for you.

It's okay to let your cat make breakfast.
My cat Pebbles makes me breakfast all
the time.

She likes to make scrambled eggs and bacon the best.

Sometimes there's cat hair in my eggs.

If I'm late for breakfast, she'll eat all the bacon.

What she really makes well is oatmeal.
Pebbles loves putting milk in things.

Sometimes she puts too much milk in my oatmeal.

On cold mornings, Pebbles bakes muffins.

The oven makes the whole kitchen warm.
It's a great place for a catnap.

But NEVER let your cat

make LUNCH for you.

One time Pebbles made a peanut butter and jelly sandwich for me to take to school.

She had to use her paws to spread the peanut butter and jelly because she can't hold a knife.

All day I was so hungry, thinking about that sandwich.

When lunch finally came, I hurried to the
lunchroom and took a gigantic bite out of
my sandwich.

My friends knew something was wrong
because I started making funny faces.

When I lifted the bread, what did I find?

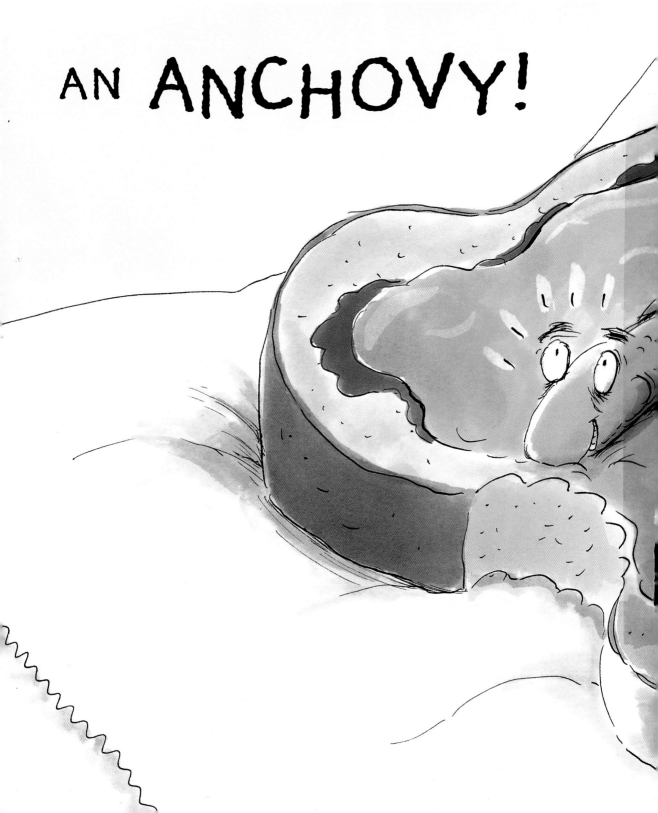

Right in the
middle of my
SANDWICH!

Only a cat would think an anchovy tastes good with peanut butter and jelly. Pebbles thinks anchovies taste good with everything! Yuck!

Imagine my surprise when I found out that nobody wanted to trade sandwiches with me.

They still remembered the mouse
sandwich I had the day before.

That's why I say never—
                and I mean never ever—
let your cat make lunch for you.

And that's the end of our tail.

Text copyright © 1999 by Lee Harris
Illustrations copyright © 1999 by Debbie Tilley

Tricycle Press
P.O. Box 7123
Berkeley, CA 94707
www.tenspeed.com

Book design by Catherine Jacobes
Typeset in Regular Joe

 Library of Congress Cataloging-in-Publication Data
Harris, Lee, 1961–
    Never let your cat make lunch for you / Lee Harris;
    pictures by Debbie Tilley.
        p. cm.
    Summary: Pebbles the cat is great at cooking breakfast, but a
    disaster when it comes to fixing lunch.
    ISBN 1-883672-80-5
    [1. Cookery—Fiction. 2. Food—Fiction. 3. Cats—Fiction.]
    I. Tilley, Debbie, ill. II. Title.
PZ7.H24213Ne 1999
[E]—dc21   98-51999
                                                 CIP
                                                 AC

First printing, 1999.

Printed in Hong Kong
1 2 3 4 5 6 — 03 02 01 00 99